Raffi Songs to Read™

ONE LIGHT, ONE SUN

Illustrated by Eugenie Fernandes

Crown Publishers, Inc., New York

Text copyright © 1988 by Troubadour Learning, a division of Troubadour Records Ltd.
Illustrations copyright © 1988 by Eugenie Fernandes.

Published by Crown Publishers, Inc. a Random House company, 225 Park Avenue
South, New York, New York 10003
CROWN is a trademark of Crown Publishers, Inc.
RAFFI SONGS TO READ and SONGS TO READ are trademarks of Troubadour
Learning, a division of Troubadour Records Ltd.
Manufactured in Singapore

Library of Congress Cataloging-in-Publication Data
Raffi.   One light, one sun.
Summary: Three families discover that despite outward differences, they are really
very much alike.
    1. Children's songs—Texts.   [1. Songs.   2. Family life—Fiction.   3. Brotherliness—
Fiction]
I. Eugenie, ill.   II. Title
PZ8.3.R124On 1987   87-22256
ISBN: 0-517-56785-7 (trade)
0-517-57644-9 (pbk.)

Originally published in hardcover in 1988

First paperback edition: February, 1990

10 9 8 7 6 5 4 3 2

Front photo © David Street
Back photo © Patrick Harbron

One light, one sun,

One sun lighting everyone.

One world turning,

One world turning everyone.

One world, one home,

One world
home for everyone

One dream,
one song,

One song heard by everyone.

One love,
one heart,

One heart
warming everyone.

One hope,
one joy,

One love filling everyone.

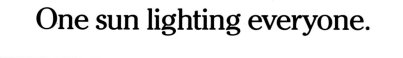

One sun lighting everyone.

One light warming everyone.

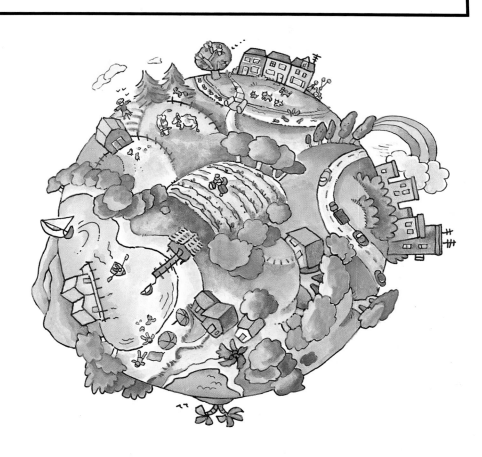

ONE LIGHT, ONE SUN

Flowing

Words & music by Raffi

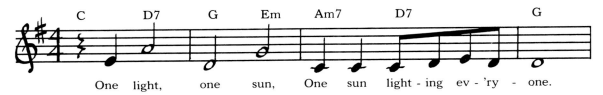

One light, one sun, One sun light - ing ev - 'ry - one.

One world turn - ing, One world turn - ing ev - 'ry - one.

2. One world, one home,
   One world home for everyone.
   One dream, one song,
   One song heard by everyone.

3. One love, one heart,
   One heart warming everyone.
   One hope, one joy,
   One love filling everyone.